Just Right for Christmas

For Adrian
B. B.

To my niece Gracie, with love
R. B.

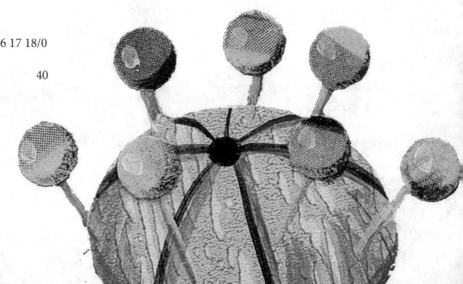

ISBN 978-0-545-64468-6

Text copyright © 2011 by Birdie Black. Illustrations copyright © 2011 by Rosalind Beardshaw. All rights reserved. Published by Scholastic Inc., 557 Broadway, New York, NY 10012, by arrangement with Candlewick Press. SCHOLASTIC and associated logos are trademarks and/or registered trademarks of Scholastic Inc.

12 11 10 9 8 7 6 5 4 3 2 1   13 14 15 16 17 18/0

Printed in the U.S.A.   40

First Scholastic printing, November 2013

This book was typeset in Cantoria MT.
The illustrations were done in mixed media.

Just Right for Christmas

Birdie Black

illustrated by

Rosalind Beardshaw

SCHOLASTIC INC.

It was Christmas Eve, and snow was falling as the king strolled around the market. What should he see but a huge roll of beautiful bright-red cloth.

"Oooh!" he said. "That cloth is so red and soft and Christmassy! It would be just right for a grand cloak for the princess!" And so he bought it and took it back to his castle.

In the castle, the king's sewing maids snipped and sewed and snipped and sewed, and by lunchtime, they had made a beautiful long cloak for the princess.
The king was delighted.

He wrapped it up in golden paper and silver ribbon.
"What shall we do with the scraps?"
one of the sewing maids asked.
"Oh, just bundle them up and put them outside
the back door," said the king.

Jenny, the castle's kitchen maid, had finished work for
the day. What should she see on her way home but
a big bundle of beautiful bright-red scraps.
"Oooh!" she said. "That cloth is so red and soft
and Christmassy! It would be just right
to make a jacket for my ma!"

When Jenny got home,
she snipped and sewed and
snipped and sewed, and . . .

by dinnertime, she'd made
a pretty red jacket
for her ma.

She was very happy, and she wrapped it up in red paper with a green ribbon.

Then she bundled up the little scraps and put them outside the back door so her ma wouldn't see them.

Bertie Badger trotted past Jenny's house.
What should he see but a little bundle of beautiful
bright-red scraps.
"Oooh!" he said. "That cloth is so red and soft and
Christmassy! It would be just right to make a hat for my pa!"

When Bertie got home,
he snipped and
sewed . . .

and snipped
and sewed, and . . .

by the time the clock
was striking six . . .

he'd made a nice
red hat for his pa.

He smiled as he wrapped
it up in some brown paper
and tied it with string.

Then he bundled up the
tiny scraps and put them
outside the back door.

Samuel Squirrel bounded past
Bertie's house. Suddenly, he stopped.
What should he see but a tiny bundle of
beautiful bright-red scraps.
"Oooh!" he said. "That cloth is so red and
soft and Christmassy! It would be just right
to make a pair of gloves for my wife!"

When Samuel got home, he snipped and
sewed and snipped and
sewed, and . . .

by the time the moon was
rising, he'd made a beautiful
pair of gloves for his wife.

He wrapped them in a leaf
and tied up the parcel with
a piece of dried grass.

"It's just as well I've made her something
to keep her hands warm," he said.
"This winter wind is so chilly!"
A gust picked up the tiny scrap of red cloth that
was left over and blew it out his window,
where it fluttered to the snowy ground.

It was nearly midnight when Milly Mouse
plodded past Samuel's house.
She was tired and cold, and the snow was falling on her
ears and whiskers. She had been looking for a nut to give
to little Billy for Christmas, but she couldn't find one.

As she passed the bottom of Samuel's tree,
she saw something red sticking out of the snow.
What could it be?
It was the tiny scrap of cloth!
"Oooh!" she said. "That cloth is so soft and
red and Christmassy. It would be just right
to make a scarf for my Billy!"

Billy was asleep when Milly got
home. She snipped
and sewed and . . .

snipped and sewed,
and by the time the candle had
burned low, she'd made a
cozy scarf for Billy.

She didn't have anything to wrap it in, but she folded it carefully
and put it under her tiny sprig of Christmas tree.

On Christmas morning,
the princess opened her
huge gold present.

And Jenny's ma opened her
big red present.

And Bertie's pa opened his
small brown-paper present.

And Samuel's wife
unwrapped her leaf.

And Milly gave little Billy his scarf.
Each present was so soft and red and Christmassy and felt just right . . .

just how Christmas should feel.